WINDOWS

Navigating City Life

WINDOWS

Navigating City Life

Prose **Mark Holman**

Poems **A.L. Sutton**

Windows: Navigating City Life
Prose by Mark Holman, Poems by A.L. Sutton.

Library of Congress
Cataloging-in-Publication Data
Windows: navigating city life /; prose by Mark Holman, poems by A. L. Sutton.
Printed in the United States of America

ISBN: 978-0-9967582-5-3

www.anointedlifepublishing.com

Dedication

To my Grandmother (Bettie Valley) whose God given wisdom, love, and not sparing the rod kept me above the war-like dangers of living in South Central Los Angeles.

A.L. Sutton

By land, east or west, north or
south, by sky, all this journey's ours,
minds open, hearts flying high,
these windows the soul's eye

A.L. Sutton

Contents

Preface

My uncle and I first considered working together on *Windows* when I had just returned from Italy in 1994. He wanted me to edit poems he had written. I told him the poems could stand on their own but that they could also be woven into a story of recollections as a protagonist journeyed through Los Angeles, Calif. on public transportation. Needless to say, I became that protagonist and coined the prose here as I logged hundreds of miles of bus and light rail trips through metropolitan Los Angeles. I was inspired to link the poetry and prose as I remembered a Middle Ages author, Boethius, we studied at Harvard in *The Consolation of Philosophy*, a Menippean Satire that regularly alternates prose and verse.

Mark Anthony Holman
Portland, Oregon

Staring out of the window of his studio apartment in his three-story high-rise (at least that's what he called the old crumbling building on the east side), Teddy was checking out the landscape below. The corner liquor store was to the right. Then there was the empty lot to the left and another one straight ahead. What was once a furniture store was now just a burnt out memory of the Watts Riot of some twenty years earlier.

Against this backdrop of despair, he catches an occasional Beemer, Benz, or Lexus zooming by, going north or south on Broadway. He doesn't stare too hard at people walking down the street. You never know when a fool might get stupid and try to pop a cap 'cause he thought you were staring him down too hard.

Teddy, Teddy, The-o-dore! Dang it boy, you better answer me! He could still hear his mother calling him now. No, this time he wasn't leaning too far out of the window. That voice was all in his mind; yesteryear. This is his world now. No parents. No loud-butt brothers and sisters to share space with him. It was just Teddy and his view below. He needed to get the best view possible so that he could begin to process this stuff.

Is that Yolanda walking by? Last year she claimed she was carrying his baby. *But you never know. Women are always trying to hook you. You can never be too sure.* Word was, she had attempted to get rid of the baby, but her mom had stopped her. Teddy had tried to act as if he didn't care, but inside he thanked God that the attempt had not been successful.

Deep down he knows that baby is his, and he's a little proud, even if it might have been too much responsibility for a 19 year-old. That's the past. He's 20 now and…*better catch that bus to work.*

IT

It looked to be a question mark
The size of an infant's hand
Still it felt the awful pain
It couldn't understand

It survived
Never to know why
A mother cursed it
And begged it to die

Its birthday was cold and loveless
But it could finally be seen
Not only was it alive
She was beautiful little human being

Now she is swelling
With an it of her own
And she's having problems
Giving it the love she's never known

Teddy glanced to his left, yawning and thinking about the drive-by where he almost got smoked just a couple of days ago. He found it harder and harder to call this place his neighborhood. He spent most of his time in transit blending in with the other tired faces forming a collage of urban despair. *Damn, it's too early to be makin' this trip for a rinky dink little job. Hell, with the money you spent on bus fare and time wasted in traffic jams, you really were just makin' a few dollars over minimum wage.*

    With all the time he spent away from his neighborhood, when Teddy did hit the streets, people sometimes looked at him like he was a stranger. C-Dog tried to smoke him last week. Looking back, it was just another low-key crap game, right? *But why do fools always try to hold onto the money when they crap out? You can't hit seven, five times in a row and expect to win the next five rolls, too. Damn fools always trying to dis you in front of the other homies. Sometimes you gotta beat 'em down.*

Teddy didn't see the 69 Impala that pulled up on the other side of the street last week. He didn't see the sawed-off muzzle sticking out of the back seat window. He didn't see the 12 gauge pellets that sprayed the barbershop window behind him, but he did feel the searing pain of the lead pellets that lodged in his shoulder. He did hear the tires peeling off layers of rubber as the car sped off. The sour smell of the burnt rubber seemed to mix with the sweet smell of his bloody shoulder, still hot from the little metal balls that had exploded out of the sawed-off barrel just seconds before.

And now, from his window, Teddy could see another scene being played out behind the laundromat across the street. *Some more crap talking. Some more cheating. Could you blame a brother for just tryin' to hustle?*

Nothing personal, but Teddy, over his young years, had developed a love/hate relationship with the hustlers/gangbangers and their victims.

HATE

Hate is just a feeling
Hot, it burns every cell of the body
Instantly
It overpowers the good
Within seconds
It breaks the fragile restraints of love
Free, for the moment
It runs unchecked
But there is little to fear,
For good is the human mountain
And hate, seasonal, is only the rain

Here we go with this plain wrap, two boxes for a dollar, can't never stay crispy in milk, soggy cereal, Yolanda thought as she read the advertisement supplement in the paper while sitting in her usual seat behind the bus driver. She was lucky she boarded at the beginning of the line because the bus was already nearly full after making just two stops on, what was for her, a 10-mile trip. At least this was the weekend, so she only had to work for four hours.

Since she moved out of Teddy's place, Yolanda was doing her best to make ends meet. But that's harder than hard when you have a new baby and no ends. It was just 30 minutes ago that the cornflake ritual had played itself out. Then, Yolanda's baby chewed on the mushy morning meal while milk dribbled down his chin.

CORNFLAKES

Sometimes Yolanda forgot to buy baby food and sometimes she ran out of money. To make do, Yolanda would take a spoonful and save a little bit for her baby. That was how they always did it two days before she got her paycheck.

The check had a way of disappearing after she paid her sister to babysit, forked over $625 for rent, paid off the interest on her credit card bills, and made her trips to the fast food places around the corner from her place.

This was just another Saturday morning for Yolanda. It began at 5 a.m. with cartoons and of course all the commercials about all the newest cereals, which hadn't changed (except for maybe name, shape, and price) since she was a kid. Always the same: Sugar-coated pieces of wheat, corn, or rice that left a sour taste in your mouth when you put the bowl up to your lips to drink the grayish milk that penetrated right through the crunch coating and changed colors. Soggy little flakes flopping around in your spoon before you took another bite. The bus lurched forward and chugged on to the next stop.

CORNFLAKES

It's cornflakes, kids,
For every morning meal
Load 'em with sugar
And wonder how they feel

Mother's kind of busy
And Daddy is, too
So let's let television
Tell 'em what to do

Sugar-coated nuggets
Loved by lions and bears
Preferred by little human beings
Served by those who care

Tomorrow's kids
Get something new
A breakfast cereal
For supper, too

Teddy saw a group of 12 and 13 year-olds walking to the bus stop in front of the laundromat. It was another Saturday morning; another Pop Warner football game. They had their football pads; carrying the shoulder pads draped over their helmets while using the face masks as handles.

Those were the days. When Teddy was playing, he would ride to games and ride home on the same bus. He always had the same driver, Andre, both going and coming. Every Saturday, Teddy faced the same dilemma. How was he going to tell Andre that he had never met his father when Andre asked him if his parents were going to the game?

Teddy usually lied and said his parents would meet him at the game because they didn't want to get there too early. But explaining the return trip, alone on the bus, was always the hard part. How was Teddy supposed to tell Andre that his mother was always too hung over from partying on Friday nights to even think about dragging her tired self out of bed at 10 a.m. just to see him run up and down a grass field, especially when it was going to cost her almost a dollar to wash his funky uniform?

The bus pulled off, pouring just a little more exhaust into the already stagnant morning air. It was now seven years later, on a different bus, that Teddy remembered you can't miss what you never had.

I never missed my Daddy
Can't miss what you never had
But sometimes I dream he's around
The most wonderful of all the dads

He hugs me all the time
Calls me his little man
And tells me very special things
Only guys can understand

We go to lots of football games
Eat hot dogs, yell, and cheer
Dad showed me how to throw a punch
And explained all men have fear

In my dream if my Dad left me
I'd die from being sad
So I guess I'm really lucky
Can't miss what I never had

TAGGING

Yolanda hated going through this part of town. Since she had moved away from Teddy's, she didn't like to remind herself of all the dreams deferred and dead-end hopes that could only be painted on the canvas of somebody else's garage or picket fence. These were the walls, fences, and faces of Teddy's neighborhood.

The little boy she saw scrawling code on the wall that looked like 83 187 Bounty Hunter, didn't realize that he was no longer hidden by the cover of darkness. At 6 a.m. you can make out a few things, especially if you've been seeing them day in and day out for nearly two years.

Taggers—you kind of wonder what makes them think their scrawl will last. Posterity for them is a day, two days, or maybe a week; until the wall is painted over or their tag is crossed out by some rival.

Taggers, maybe they are just a reflection of life. If this is a world where you can get half-hour resolutions and all of life's melodrama on TV, why not go for some quick and easy fame of your own? Just don't hit up a freeway bridge or a rival gang's 'hood.

Yolanda shook her head as the bus passed by the yards and yards of walls abutting the railroad tracks. Each one had something scribbled on it. *Taggers.*

TAGGING

It's more than a game
This tagging
It's a doomed dog's tail,
Still wagging

Our deprived and undisciplined children
Depicting a future of horror
As perhaps it can only be seen
By these owners of tomorrow

Tagging reflects
The mistakes of our past
Where the value of good
Was too simple and not allowed to last

Tagging is part of
But surely not the whole problem
Solutions exist
But is jail really one of them?

There is always some fool on the bus talking about the latest topic flooding the airways of the talk shows during the week. Last week it was latch-key kids. This week: political correctness. Like last week, there was a prophet of Geraldo giving everybody the 411. Yolanda looked over her shoulder from time to time to hear the latest bus prophet. As always and like all the others, everyone from the rear of the bus to the front could hear him. On this day, Yolanda didn't know which one was louder, this guy's mouth or the hum of the bus engine as they pulled off from the curb.

P.C.—another one of those cliché terms that gets lost in the shuffle after a couple of years. Quality time! Word up! Yea, that's the ticket. All these little sayings that rise from the ashes of our common experience and like a Phoenix, just fly away and take on an aura of their own while we are left wondering how the terms came about in the first place. But P.C. seemed to have an emptiness unmatched by any of those other terms. If you don't want to offend somebody, then resort to that P.C. vocabulary, the kind her UCLA-educated supervisor would use. All this snap about Asian instead of Oriental, African-American instead of Black, using "he" half the time and "she" the other half when describing something that was definitely masculine or feminine.

P.C. just sounded like a lukewarm way of dealing with the intensity of your feelings. *Yeah, put all the P.C. people in a big ditch with those who were spending quality time doing lunch with somebody.* It was a good thing Yolanda was getting off in two stops. She didn't know how long she could deal with this fool blabbermouth.

P. C.

P.C. for the week
Is the order of the day
P.C. is doing nothing
While they take your Mom away

P.C. is the smart not seeing
When seeing gets in the way
P.C. is making a stand

Not based on how you feel
P.C. is simply being P.C.
Even if the facts aren't real

It was certainly not P.C.
That made America great
I believe the Founding Fathers
Would regard P.C. as fake

Sometimes Teddy felt like he was winding his way through an above-ground maze. The streets of L.A. were mean in his neighborhood. There were Minotaurs waiting around eerie corners—tricks, pimps, hustlers, whores, little 'hood rats, and gangbangers; all waiting to catch you slippin'.

But there were saints, too. The old woman crossing the street holding her grandchildren's hands, or Mr. Simms standing in front of his fish store that somehow was passed over during the riots. Maybe his little cardboard "black owned" sign in the front window did mean something to somebody.

Yeah, there was Mr. Simms, cleaning the sidewalk, although it would become filthy again at 3:30 when all the school kids walked by dropping their candy wrappers and spitting out their bubble gum.

The inside of the bus was spic and span, too, but outside, the filth and scratches on the window, which Teddy was peering through, seemed to distort the winos sitting on milk crates at the corner opposite the small church. Thunderbird dreams riding in on the night train lane; a game of bones has gotta be in the mix.

The streets of South Central
Are covered with blood
The reasons are obvious
If you live in the 'hood

Education is lacking
And jobs are, too
My, oh, my,
What's a young man to do

In a land of plenty
And justice for a few?
Those without
Have nothing to lose

"Hey, what's happenin', chief?" Teddy greeted Larry as he hopped on the bus. Every now and then he and Larry would bump into each other on the bus. Usually, they tripped off the stuff they used to do when they were growing up. Teddy placed his Nike sports bag on the floor and moved over into the empty seat as Larry plopped down next to him. As they exchanged greetings, Larry pointed out a parking meter attendant on the other side of the street.

"Man, remember we used to hit up those parking meters?" Larry chuckled.

"Yeah man. How can I forget?" nodded Teddy. "A screwdriver and some adrenaline. Man, that's all we needed and we'd be hooked up with candy money for the rest of the week," spurted Teddy as the bus pulled off, and he looked at the meter attendant placing a little canister in a machine that he was wheeling around on something that looked like a portable luggage carrier.

They used to pop the locks on parking meters with a screwdriver that Teddy "borrowed" from his mother's boyfriend's toolbox. They had removed most of the canisters from the meters so the change would just spill out when the belly of the meter opened up. Usually they managed to close the meter up, so unsuspecting motorists would use it over and over again. Sometimes they'd break the lock and the meter door wouldn't close. This was always a welcome to the drivers who parked in those spaces. If the meter was broken, they couldn't put money in it. Teddy noticed the same cars were always parked at the spaces with the broken meters—the cars that were tore down and bashed up like his mother's boyfriend's car.

So Teddy and Larry reminisced about their days as Robin Hoods. They provided a few people with free parking, and they collected a little change to buy Doritos, Now & Laters, and ice cream sandwiches. Naw, they weren't stealing, just getting over.

I steal because I want to
Not because I need
I steal because I'm mad at you
Just like you're mad at me

I steal because it's popular
I see it all the time
Only they steal millions
Most of it yours and mine

Both Teddy and Larry had been working fulltime for the past few months. Of course they always did some extra work on the side, but now it was always legit. Larry was a security guard over at the movie studios in Culver City. Teddy drove the Avis courtesy van at LAX. "You gotta love being a chauffeur after being chauffeured to work on a 60-seat limo like this. Hey, it's all in a day's work," he used to kid Larry.

Somehow Teddy got a kick out of being the first black driver that most out-of-towners met when they came into L.A. He would trip off of some people's amazement that he could carry on a conversation without sounding like a gangsta rapper. At the same time, he would be amazed by the accents and, at times bug-eyed enthusiasm of those coming to L.A. for the first time.

"Man," began Larry, "I was chasin' this little sucker off the lot the other day—you know the typical starving artist type posing as a pizza boy and using that sorry line so he could sneak onto the lot and 'network.' Well, this little sucker got pissed off when I told him his game was weak, and he started cussin' me out. When I went to escort him off the property, he took a swing at me and practically… Hey Teddy," Larry interrupted himself in the middle of one of his many work adventure stories, "look at that raggedy dude across the street." He pointed toward a young man in a Rastafarian cap who was hawking foot-long aluminum covered sticks to passers-by.

"Man, that's Winslow from 42nd street, ain't it?"

Visibly shook, Teddy slowly nodded in affirmation. "I remember he used to clock a fat grip when he was in the business. Now look at his rusty butt; reduced to this."

"Yeah, man. No gun. No dope. No terrorizing people no more. Yeah, man, I guess a hollow point in the backside'll calm you down," sighed Larry. The bus rolled on.

The boy next door is dealing
But here no one is caring
It's understood
Dope in the 'hood's a temp job
And the money's slamming
Just yesterday
He was playing in school, planning
And bragging as young boys do
But he was never a part
Of the master plan
It's where trickle down ends
That his life begins
The boy next door is now the man
Serving the night
With a gun in his hand

Yolanda was running a little early and thought about taking a stroll for a couple of blocks to the next bus stop where she had to transfer. *You spent just as much time setting in traffic as you did walking to the next stop*…and she did have to tighten up, so those stretch marks would finally disappear. She reached to push the black plastic-covered strip and started to get up when she was rushed from both the front and behind by other passengers vying for a seat. *Freak this.* She decided to ride on to the next stop. Yes, this was another part of the early morning drama on the #8.

Yolanda hated this street. Here, three years ago, she saw her first drive-by shooting. She and Teddy were walking home from a date when a '76 Monte Carlo pulled up alongside some boys on the other side of the street. She remembered the yelling, the explosion, and the red rags hanging out of the window as the murderers drove off.

This particular corner marked a divide. Just on the other side of the street began View Park, and it seemed as if someone had put up a sign that said don't even think about calling this place South Central, L.A. The houses were bigger, the streets didn't have potholes, the lawns were greener, and you could see nice cars swooping down the streets all the time. This was where she worked four years ago. In fact, she first met Teddy at a little soul food restaurant on the View Park side of the street.

There was a good side of the tracks and a bad side. Funny how this divide existed even in the black neighborhoods. But don't ever forget: you could get smoked on either side of the street if you had on the wrong color. One more stop and Yolanda would be transferring. One more stop and two more miles to work.

With weapons of death in hand
Blue brothers are stalking the badlands

With nothing to claim for fame
Blue brothers will kill again

The enemy of choice is red
Because of red, a blue is dead

The loss of life is endless
And the reasons stupid and senseless

With weapons of death in hand
Red brothers are stalking the badlands

"Crazy fool!" The bus driver yelled as he swerved to avoid Smodarita. "They need to put him out to pasture…Get 'im off the streets before he makes somebody kill him." Teddy wasn't surprised that the bus hadn't run down Smodarita, the neighborhood panhandler. If anyone had nine lives, it had to be this cat. Rita had taken to living out of a basket. He strapped two baskets together, one with the cans, copper wiring, and other junk he had rummaged that day and the other with his rolled up cardboard crib and rags and stuff he needed to set up against the night.

Now, Smodarita was okay when he pulled his carts slowly, but if he got in hurry, then the rear basket would sway like the container on a big rig making a wide turn. This day he was moving with some pep to his step when he decided to cut out in the street just as Teddy's bus was going by. "Smodarita, he ain't going nowhere, baby," chuckled an old woman who was a regular rider on this line. "So you might as well get used to us swerving around him, baby," she admonished the bus driver. The bus crossed the tracks of the new Blue Line Metro station and continued east.

GLUE

There stands the old plow horse
A sad look on his face
He still nods and forces a smile
But it's his eyes that really speak

Times are changing
And he can't keep up with the pace
He knows he's just an old plow horse
Trapped in a thoroughbred's race

No rewards for past service
It's all gone down a worker's drain
The farmer smiles but warns
He needs horses that are trained

They placed him in the far field
Where all the grass was brown
With nothing at all to do
But simply stand around

His sad eyes tell the story
What he believes now to be true
That old plow horses, if boiled alive
Can make the most wonderful glue

Teddy got off the bus and transferred to the Blue Line. L.A. was so proud of this— its first light rail system since the days of the Red Line in the '50s. Pulling up to the Watts station at 103rd, he could see the famous Watts Tower to the right. *Yep, one man's junk is always another one's treasure*, he thought, as the theme from *Sanford and Son* played in his head.

But the true treasure for him was those two older women sitting on the bench as they waited to catch the train to Long Beach. They must have been in their 70s and seemed to be enjoying each other's company as they waved their hands spiritedly while conversing. *Two gray foxes and looking good*, he thought.

How different that scene was from the one he saw yesterday. An old bag lady had boarded the Blue Line and stretched out across three seats. Her evil glances and pungent smell dared anyone to come within two feet of her. She was just another lost and forgotten soul; left alone. Maybe she was a victim of the Reagan trickle-down theory. Maybe she suffered because of the indifference of her king. "I got a bunk education, double-digit inflation, can't take the train to the job," Teddy flashed back on Grandmaster Flash and the Furious Five's "Message" for a second, but the train of questions continued.

How could you stop giving a damn about your mother, grandmother, or even the old lady next door? How could you become so caught up in your own thing that you forget that life revolves around others, too? Nobody asks to be forgotten, although they often ask to be just left alone.

*Amid the decay and crimes Of South
Central
An old woman cowers alone
Frightened by violence
Beneath her only window*

*Her face reflects the trouble
And problems of our time
And though she rarely sees them
Her kids are on her mind*

*Her years of work and servitude
Have taken a heavy toll
And her painful, old arthritic limbs
Won't always do as they're told*

*She never asks for a helping hand
Content to do the best she can*

ALONE

She knows humanity
Has passed her by
Still, stubborn in her pride,
She waits alone to die

Although Larry was still on the bus heading downtown, Teddy continued to recollect their conversation. Teddy was puzzled. Larry didn't curse anymore. Although he used to say, MF or SOB, now he wouldn't let anything stronger than "ass" cross his lips.

"Man, when did you stop cussin'?" Teddy had asked, a bit surprised. "Cause I've been checking you out for the past few seconds and I'm thinking that the rough edges got smoothed out when you were in the County. So, what's up?"

Larry shrugged his shoulders and explained, "I won't say that I got saved and sanctified, and I don't sell bean pies, either. The rough edges, well, they're a little smoother. But I will say that staring at those bars day in and day out for a month and a half, because of some small stuff, helped me to get a little more focused on responsibilities I had. Responsibilities I wasn't keeping. Man, my kids don't need to hear that kinda stuff, all that cussin'. And my woman don't need to hear it, either. It's a trip, but with so much negativity being served up to us in this part of town, at least I feel I can make a little bit of a difference. Add a bit of a positive vibe around this camp."

A positive vibe is just what the place needs, thought Teddy. The train hummed along the track at speeds that were unheard of on the congested Harbor freeway. But the people on the freeway didn't know about life along the corridor on the train. It didn't even seem to register with those people from Orange County traveling north on the 110, hermetically sealed in their sedans. Their only care was getting to and from the smoggy center of the city. They must have known that with eight out of ten of them riding alone in their cars, there was bound to be more traffic. They must have known that parking their cars in Long Beach and riding the Blue Line into downtown L.A. was much quicker than maneuvering through traffic jams for an hour or so, but maybe it was just too real for them to be so close to city life. *In the city, but not of it. Yeah, that's what they are.*

The houses whizzing by seemed to meld into one dirty pastel and gray streak as the train went past the Firestone station. In two more stops Teddy would be at Vernon, where he would make his second-to-last transfer.

The writing on the walls and fences had become Mexican gangbanger script. He heard more chatter in Spanish on the train as Salvadorans and Mexicans boarded. One day he was going to have to get his Spanish back up to snuff so he could get that promotion on his job.

Somewhere in America,
Little kids are singing
But here, where my homies live,
The gunshots are a ringin'

Somewhere in America,
Exist communities of happy people
But here, where my homies live,
Life is hopeless, deadly and simple

Somewhere in America,
ABCs are learned in school
But here, where my homies live,
Staying alive is the Golden Rule

SOMEWHERE

Somewhere in America,
There is talk of truth and justice
But here, where my homies live,
The talk is about who's being busted

Somewhere in America,
There is support for other nations
But here, where my homies live,
It's a desperate situation

Somewhere in America,
The dream is still alive
But here, where my homies live,
The dream has long since died

Later for all these basket-pushin', panhandlin' fools, Yolanda thought. For some reason, at this stop, the same old woman would curse Yolanda out, just on general principle. Just on G.P. Yolanda was young. She was old. Yolanda had a job. She had none and had to depend on handouts. Yolanda was pretty; with caramel-colored skin and big brown eyes. The old woman was crusty and dirty with blotches all over her face and slits that showed yellowish bloodshot eyes. Every morning it was her duty to look at Yolanda and suck her teeth disdainfully.

Maybe Yolanda first pissed her off when the woman asked for some money and Yolanda said that every spare cent she had was needed to buy food and diapers for her baby. How was Yolanda to know that the woman had lost two babies at childbirth and saw her teenaged son gunned down on her front porch, in cold blood, just a few years ago? How was Yolanda supposed to know this woman had just stopped caring after losing her husband to colon cancer, one son to the cancer of random violence spreading across the city, and her other babies to God knows what stresses?

Yolanda looked at the buses going in opposite directions. Each time she followed a bus, her eyes would inevitably meet with those bloodshot yellow slits of the bag woman. *Why couldn't she just go somewhere? Why is this bench and this stop so special? She's like a stray dog, coming to piss on the same pole every day.*

Yolanda didn't know that this was the last corner where the woman and her husband had walked together.

In the nineties, people,
It's all about respect
Everybody wants it
Though most haven't earned it yet

The few who claim they have it
Say it's impossible to get
While those who have to do without
Believe you're born with it

There's only one rule
In the nineties pertaining to respect:
You should never give
What you never get

"Man, I looked out those dingy bars and every day I saw somebody who looked like somebody I knew. I heard jokes that sounded like the ones the winos around the corner from my house used to tell when they were playing dominoes. Towards the end, I would pump iron. I'd walk around standin' tall. You know, it's like M.L.K. used to say, 'A man can't ride your back unless it's bent,' and I didn't want any of those fools thinkin' I was slinking around and was game for the okey-doke. Naw, I was nobody's fool."

"Towards the end, I also started rappin' with this female guard. Her older brothers had been in the County and later in Folsom. She knew the ins and outs, but I found it strange that her family was on both sides of the law. She didn't have to be there.

'But if I can touch one life,' she used to say, 'then that's one less person who might get killed in a prison fight over something stupid like which soap to watch on television.' "

"Man, towards the end, I started to see too much of myself and my frustrations in there. I knew I had to have my stuff straight because I didn't want to even find out what the next step would be like."

Yeah, too much dumb stuff, sighed Teddy as he thought about the last part of his conversation with Larry. Teddy was winding his way to his last transfer point, and it seemed like more and more yoked dudes were getting on the bus. He shouldn't jump to conclusions by thinking they just had institutional bodies, but hey, there were no Gold's Gyms around here.

STRANGER

There's a stranger wearing
My brother's face
I smile
But his smile has been replaced

I'm amazed at how straight
And tall he stands
In retrospect
A broken man

His future already
A part of his past
He is the hopeful
Surrounded by the hopeless mass

I predict his future
To soon be one of angry violence
If only I could make him see
The stranger, him, is also me

"Man, pass that on over here. Gimme a sip of that 40 ounce, G."

"Naw, man, I just gave yo ass some. Hold up, fool, hold up!"

It was strange seeing gangsters on the bus. The bus was a vulnerable place for them. Unless they were jackin' somebody, they were sitting ducks for somebody who might want to walk on the bus and smoke them. They were easy game for somebody who wanted to walk up to the window and empty a clip. Teddy had seen it happen.

As the bus passed by Winchell's, Teddy laughed to himself. *Glazed pigs.* But what could you do? They weren't all bad. At least they provided gangster population control sometimes.

But drugs and easy money make strange bed buddies. You never knew if you were selling to an undercover crooked cop who might have gone undercover just to cover his tracks, or if you were making a legit deal. Too bad Larry didn't know that three months ago. At least he knows it now.

Well, it's an all-out war
That's what it's like for me
They wanna put me down
But I ain't going for it, G

I'm gonna rise up
'Cause I ain't no fool
No way I'm gonna win
Playing by these kinda rules

Poor people working
And the rich getting paid

I'm not my Daddy
And I don't understand
Why it's so hard for me
To catch up with the man

GANGSTER

If I get sick, G
I ain't got no place to go
Without insurance
They won't treat me anymo'

It ain't no game
I need cash, G
I got bills times babies
And people looking for me

So now you know
It's a different set of rules
Man, when you get yours,
You're gonna get mine too

I don't want to be a gangster
But since that's the way it is
I'm not strapped for playing, G
It takes all of this to live

The Metrorail rounded the corner, heading towards the Washington station. Yolanda's mother used to go to classes at Trade Technical College, right across from the Washington station. Across the street was the Burger King where Yolanda's eighth grade boyfriend had beaten up a little wanna-be Crip much to the delight of all the cheering patrons and the regulars who had seen the wanna-be bullying other kids.

Now the train was filled with police officers, protecting and serving; as they monitored the shiny, new Blue Line. No graffiti. No bums panhandling. No loud high school kids smackin' gum or spilling food all over the place. Yeah, the new Metrorail was a far cry from the buses she used to catch to Crenshaw High just a couple of years ago.

THE LINE

"This has gotta to be the safest line in town," joked an old black man sitting by the policemen. But as another passenger looked up at the six policemen standing at the exit of the train, she didn't know if she felt safe or not. They looked the same to her as those policemen who made her lie face down on the ground when they mistook her house for the neighborhood crack house in the heyday of Chief Daryl Gates' battering ram campaign.

The also looked the same as the policemen who had picked up Yolanda's brother and dropped him off in Blood 'hood when he was banging. The cover of darkness didn't hide him from the bullet that a Rollin' 20 put in his back. That night there was nobody there to protect and serve.

The LAPD
Is not my friend
Too much like soldiers
I do comprehend

Any's a tough war
This I know well
I spent two tours in Nam
My own little hell

No, the LAPD is not my friend
But we're thankful
For the help they give
Each day over and again

Nothing personal
We both understand
There's a line in the sand
Between the 'hood and the man

The picture of Cassius Clay's TKO win over Sonny Liston, which hung on the wall of Mr. Simms' fish store, was brownish-gray. Years of fish grease covered the glass and frame. And it was only every now and then that Mr. Simms would take the picture down, tear off a piece of newspaper and dip it in water, then wipe the picture glass and frame clean.

He liked Cassius Clay. He liked a man who talked a good game and backed it up. He respected Muhammad Ali, too. But Mr. Simms identified more with the young fighter in Rome who mixed it up like a stealth tiger; the young man who sho' nuff did a number on Sonny Liston that night.

Mr. Simms fought like Cassius when those two young thugs came into his store the first time. He kicked some rump and took a bullet in the shoulder before he wrestled the gun away and shot the other hoodlum. But Mr. Simms didn't know that the little 16-year-olds would be out on the street the next summer stalking him at night and talking about how they were going to ice him. Word was out that they were supposed to get him on the Fourth of July weekend, but the next time he heard about those thugs, one had been shot 22 times and the other had been shot 52 times. It don't pay to be a Five-Deuce Crip when Bloods with Uzis get a beef with you.

Still, Mr. Simms and the other shopkeepers on his block were always watching their backs, especially after that first week of the month when times were lean for a lot of families in the hood.

THEN

Then there's
The good folk
At work, church, and school
Trying to live by those golden rules

And then the shooting starts
And they go down, too
Now you're a witness
But you're thinking about you

You know our little system
Won't keep them in jail
Justice for criminals, victims lose
Oh, well

Finally, there's you, you and me
We're part of the problem
But then
That we don't see

"Threes, pleeze!"

"Yeah, well, don't forget my dime, too!"

"Keep it comin', baby, 'cause I'm on the gravy train!"

It seemed like the domino players at the corner liquor store had nothing but time. Bill was an air traffic controller about twelve years ago, but he found out that under Reaganomics, he was expendable. Charlie had a burger joint that got burned down in the riot. Too bad he didn't have enough insurance to protect himself from the black and brown rage that was let loose thanks to some sorry policemen in the Valley and a media more concerned with fanning the flames that reporting the news.

"I gotta pass. Who holdin' all them deuces?"

"I know, man. Somebody at this table always lockin' up the game."

The other two players were homies from way back and it was always understood that they were in cahoots when the bones started slammin'. They were also in it together when they were up in Oregon cutting trees. That's before saving owls and trees pulled a better hand.

Teddy passed by this liquor store every time he transferred to the bus that took him to the airport. Every day he wondered if he were only a paycheck away from joining the bone yard crew.

Hey, the bus is coming. Among all the little torn pieces of paper in his pocket, he searched for his transfer.

Today I lost my job
And I'm not sure why
It seems the stupid job
Endangered a butterfly

All the work was stopped
Just like that
And as strangers chased butterflies
There we weeping workers sat

The government wrote they were sorry
Agreeing life's a struggle at best
They hated to end our jobs
But there were only 50 butterflies left

As the bus made a hard left at the South Central View Park divide, Teddy noticed Walky-Talky going by. As usual, he was deeply engaged in a conversation with his favorite person—himself. At first, Walky-Talky got strung out on P.C.P. Later, it was primos. Now, it's quarter rocks of crack.

His 6'2" frame no longer holds up 220 pounds of rippling muscles. Now, his skin and bones are just a hanger for clothes he got for a couple of dollars at the Salvation Army over on Vermont and Manchester. His hollowed chest can barely suck in the $5 rocks he now scrapes and scrounges for. The sad thing is that Walky-Talky was just one of the legions of crack warriors who roamed the streets of the city checking phones to see if someone had left some change in them and spying curbs in search of coins that may have dropped out of somebody's wallet. They were always on the lookout to catch somebody slippin'.

The bus traveled south on the divide and the plate glass windows on the right-hand side of the street reflected burnt out buildings on the left-hand side of the street. Fifteen more minutes and Teddy would be at work.

MESSAGE

> The *trumpeter*
> From hell has spoken
> Not only the weak
> But the strong shall be broken
>
> Unfortunates
> Left behind to cry
> Will know it's the living
> Not the dead who die
>
> Now the battle to the light
> Will most certainly become savage
> And no fathered child
> Will be allowed easy passage
>
> This message, my friends
> Is where the crack begins
> And where life as you know it
> Will most certainly end

Yolanda looked at the bus going in the opposite direction. *That looked like Teddy sitting at the back window. Naw, he didn't work on Saturday. Why would he be sitting at the back of the bus?* He always talked about how he had to give Rosa Parks her props; he preferred to stand right in front of the bus in everybody's way as they boarded, just because black people didn't have to go to the back of the bus any longer.

Teddy often got on his moral high horse but that would disappear when it was time to get high. Yolanda flashed back to the time they first smoked weed together. She remembered the munchies after. She remembered the great sex the morning after. She remembered all the times they got high. She remembered how she had stopped getting high once she got pregnant.

She remembered when Teddy started to smoke less because he said he was tired of all his money going to the weed man. Or, she wondered, was it because he was getting tired of her and wasn't ready to claim their child?

Finally Yolanda's bus screeched up and she boarded as she took her fingers out of her ears. *Ten minutes of waiting just to travel five minutes.* The tradeoff seemed unfair and she was always hustling up the stairs to get to her workstation with all the other secretaries. She sure didn't want to lose her job to one of the temps now working at the firm. With Teddy out of her mind, she jockeyed for position on the standing-room-only bus. *Ten more minutes and the day will begin.*

Alone I sit here, staring
Into the middle of the 21ˢᵗ century
My mind is racing, seeking
Seeking the compromise

A hit, no, yes
A hit, a hit, just one small hit
No, I fight it
It's all about time, this battle

Oh, God, I pray
Please, please, don't let me fail
It's only a whisper
Afraid I am of insulting my only power

A hit, it races across my mind
Lifting my head, watering my mouth
A hit, a hit, just one small hit
A hit, a hit, a hit

MINUTE

I reach down deep
Looking for the here within
I find only myself and yet,
In the reaching, a minute has passed
I'm winning by only by a minute

That scene in the movie, *Wall Street* haunted Teddy. Remembering Charlie Sheen getting hauled off to prison by officers of the Security and Exchange Commission, Teddy thought back to a line from an E.E. Cummings' poem. *Yeah, man does look into the abyss and the only thing that stops him from entering is that he sees himself among all the other craziness going on.*

That face had to be Yolanda's. Sure, he had never seen those clothes on her before, but she was always going to Nordstrom's. Nearly broke him—shopping for clothes—when they were together. Yes, that was Yolanda this time and not the Mexican woman he has seen earlier in the morning as he looked out of his apartment window. *Yeah, Larry was right. Sometimes we have to be a little less self-centered. Sometimes we have to change course because there's some scary stuff out there, man. Call it the Devil. Call it the streets. Call it that bull they call it on television. You can call it what you want to, but it's a doomed dog's tail waggin', as Mr. Simms would say.*

As the bus headed up the last stretch of Sepulveda Boulevard to the airport, Teddy looked up at the planes in landing patterns. Soon he'd be engaged in small talk with some of those people.

I looked down from my window
Amazed by what I should see
There, draped in flaming red,
Was old Satan, smiling up at me

He spoke without speaking
Calling me by name
Then he begged me to come down
& let him explain

I sat there shaking from head to toe
& even 'tho I managed to turn and go
I thought anyway
What he wanted me to know:

UNFORSEEN

There were wonderful visions
Of what my life could be
There was everything
I could possibly imagine
All of it was free

Seeing his effect in my greedy eyes
Satan turned the very streets to gold
Then made his only real mistake
By asking for my soul

Larry got off the bus and walked past the downtown hotel on his way to the homeless shelter to do his four hours of community service. He helped to clean the place. He shared war lies and fish stories with the residents. He served food and broke up the occasional fight.

There was a lot for him to be proud of. He wasn't dealing anymore. He was taking care of his family. His job at the movie studio was paying the bills and the grass he cut on Saturday afternoons bought clothes and toys for his kids. Three months out of the County and he was makin' it again. His wife drove the car because he didn't want her to have to deal with all the crazies on the busses.

There was a lot for him to be proud of today. He had stopped one guy from nearly killing himself. He had played spades with these cats who only talked about what life was going to be like once they got their lives together. *But that's the way it should be, right? Get all your stuff in order.*

THE LESSON

If ever I've learned a lesson
It's this thing called doing time
I sit, I sleep, I eat, I excrete
And kiss a badge's behind

My new friends
They're the scum of the earth
All getting their just rewards

The things we learn are simple
Easy to understand
Don't feel, don't protest
Just follow the rest

For the man with the badge is heartless
He'll sweat you, beat you
Resist and he'll kill you

THE LESSON

Nothing personal, understand
Just part I'm told of a master plan
To make you a better man

Yes, I've learned my lesson in this place
And I'm telling all my friends

I'm obeying all laws, no bad fun
I'll never come here again

Teddy realized Larry was right. As the bus pulled into parking lot C at the airport, Teddy thought about Yolanda. He wondered if she had seen him when she caught her last bus to work. He also wondered if their baby was healthy, had enough food to eat, and had enough clothes to wear.

He didn't want to leave her, but when he found out she had been playin' him while they were together, he flew off the handle. Maybe he should have forgiven her because at least she told him and he didn't have to hear it on the grapevine. Maybe he should have just left her a note telling her that since old flames never die, there was no room for him in their relationship.

Who cares if she had to abort the baby she and Paul would have had? Who cares if Paul's mother's illness forced him to go back to New Orleans? Who cares if Paul stopped calling and she thought he had died or something? Who cares that Paul had been searching for her for three months before he finally found her? Who cares if Paul didn't leave her messages because her mother never would have passed them on to her anyway? And who cares if the hardest thing Yolanda had to ever do was tell Paul, her first love, that they could never have what they had before?

No, she wasn't trying to patch things up with Paul, she was just letting him know where they stood now. She wasn't afraid to ask for his friendship since Teddy had left her.

With the thoughts of his last conversation with Yolanda still fresh in his mind after nearly a year and a half, Teddy decided he was going to "get sick" right before lunchtime today and go set things straight with her. *Yeah, Larry was right. There are some things that you can't run away from. Of course, that's my baby and not Paul's.* Teddy remembered a picture of the baby that some of Yolanda's and his friends had shown him. *It even has my eyes and my feet,* he thought. It was bound to look even more like him now.

BUT

I'm standing here alone with nothing
Doing the best I can
I could go out to rob or steal
But that's not being a man

Odds makers bet against me
It's not an easy life
But I'm moving forward anyway
Making it a fight

I hope the Lord is with me
Showing me the call
Understanding how bad I wanna come
up
Without making others fall

Yolanda was shocked when Teddy walked into her office in his Avis uniform. Since they had broken up, she didn't even know that he was working at the airport. She thought he was still in Hollywood at that electronics store.

She couldn't cause a scene right then and there by telling him to go his way, especially when he seemed so sincere when he asked her to bring the baby over so they could talk. He wanted to get his life back in order and they all needed to be together for him to do it. *Why should I give him the time of day?* She thought that she sure wasn't taking her baby to that crumbling old building, but while her coworkers looked on, she just nodded and said okay. Yes, she would meet him for lunch later. But her nod was a weak, indecisive one.

DAWN

Yolanda knew that Teddy had left work early; gotten "sick" and had one of his co-workers drop him off at her job in time to catch her before she went to lunch. He would be waiting for her at the café across the street from Fat Burgers. Maybe she would show up. Maybe she wouldn't.

Hours later, standing at Teddy's window and looking at the laundromat below seemed so alien to Yolanda. There seemed to be a crap game going on right beside the glow of a fifty-gallon tin drum that was keeping three men warm with the broken box crates burning inside of it. Standing there at the window and facing the east side of town was for Yolanda the best view she ever had of the orange glow that would take away the dawn.

DAWN

I stare in amazement and wonder
A witness to the birth of this new day
Aware of the magical power of dawn
And the role in my life that it plays

I had no guarantee
Before sleep last night
That my eyes would open again
To such a beautiful sight

I rejoice, drawing strength from
Another dawn's light
And Thank God *in advance*
For the rest of my life

Yolanda couldn't believe she had spent the night at Teddy's house. Nor could she believe her baby was sleeping in a makeshift crib that Teddy made, on the floor beside him. The dingy walls of this place reminded her of her house after her father had died. She and her mother didn't have enough energy to do everything in the house, so the walls were forgotten. "We'll paint 'em right before Aunt Lucie comes this summer." *Yeah, right.*

Teddy awakened for a moment and looked at Yolanda as she looked out of the window. He looked over at his baby, Angel. His gaze then lingered on a picture of Jesus that his mother had hung on his wall. *Maybe it's time to go to church.* With a smile, he rolled over and fell asleep again.

Don't even believe we're happy in hell
Satisfied with petty drugs
And little sidewalk deals
Determined to fail
Inborn excuses
Guns in our schools
Only a homeboy dies
Hanging with the gang thing
A coward's way out

Now some somehow get through college
That's what I'm talking about
Making a difference
Easing the pain
Never too late

Think of the children for a change
Who will guide them, if not us?

HELL'S CORNER

Education instead of violence
Peace in the 'hood
Love, respect and honor
One's greatest resource must
Always be oneself

Dare to aspire
An example is community wealth
It will not be easy
But easy doesn't make the man
There may be no heroes in this game
Surely, we'll stumble and fall
But the shame is in not getting up
Even if you have to crawl
To pass the torch of experience
And knowledge on to our sons
And daughters
On or own, we'll enhance the world
From one of Hell's forgotten corners

A.L. Sutton is a United States Marine veteran who served two tours in Vietnam.

While living in Long Beach, California, Al wrote daily, and this book is a project he penned with his nephew, Mark Holman. Al was born on March 24th, 1947, in St. Louis, Missouri. Al's mother, Geneva, only 16 years older, was like a sister and best friend, and all his life he called her *Niva* instead of *mother*. His mother figure, the lady he called *mom* and his hero, was his grandmother, Betty Valley, who he went to live with at age 12 in Los Angeles, a.k.a. South Central.

ABOUT A.L. SUTTON

Al attended L.A. schools, graduated from Thomas Jefferson High School in Feb. 1966 and along with his best friend, Rapth, joined the Marine Corps. Both found themselves in Viet Nam with Rapth being wounded by the time Al got there in December, 1966.

Al did two 13-month tours of duty in Vietnam as a UH-IE Helicopter crew chief and door gunner, returning from his last tour and getting out of the Marines in November, 1969.

In 1971, he married his first wife, Fanny. They had their first daughter, Alicia, and he began attending Los Angeles Trade Technical College. He graduated in 1973 with an A.S. degree in Aviation Tech.

Al found work as a licensed aircraft mechanic for several aviation companies until in 1989, when he began suffering from what he would later learn was P.T.S.D. and found himself on a psychiatric ward at the V.A. Hospital. It was a V.A. therapist, a few years later, who suggested he write poetry and since then, he has written his feelings in the form of poetry. His first efforts focused on Viet Nam and its ongoing impact on his friends and himself. Later, he wrote about his upbringing in his other war (also still going on) in the inner cities across America.

Mark Holman is a 38 year-old who has unique right – and left-brain accomplishments. A cum laude graduate of Harvard University, Mark was born in South Central, Los Angeles. This book, a collaboration between uncle and nephew, ties Mark's Harvard studies and prose writing to his own and his uncle's (A.L. Sutton) home turf, metropolitan Los Angeles.

Currently Mark resides in Portland, Oregon. While working and raising a family, Mark completed his graduate studies at

Portland State University, earning a Master's in Business Administration.

He is a multilingual, multicultural, and creative problem solver and consensus builder with demonstrated strengths in financial and marketing analysis, business strategy, and community outreach, Mark is accomplished in computer systems design and implementation, financial modeling, problem solving, and team building.

Though young, Mark has lived a full and varied life. He has parlayed his knowledge of foreign languages and cultures with his business acumen to find jobs in Moscow, Russia; Milan, Italy; Washington, D.C.; and Cambridge, Mass. Mark is also an accomplished Financial Analyst for the Department of Energy where he concentrates on debt repayment models.

Mark always has a foot in the arts world by either writing his own pieces or coordinating activities of the Cascade Festival of African Films in Portland, Oregon, where he currently serves as the Festival's president and where he is currently working on a fictional piece about life in the Soviet Union during the fall of communism.

Mark Holman, Casa de Piedra 1986, is a Business Process Analyst and Compliance Specialist, for Bonneville Power Administration (BPA). He's has specialized in the following areas: Standards of Conduct, Reliability, and Equal Employment Opportunity. He has also worked at BPA as a Financial Analyst and a Computer Systems Analyst. He holds an MBA with a focus on Innovation and Technology from Portland State University. He is a cum laude graduate of Harvard College where he majored in Russian and Soviet Studies. He is fluent in Russian language.

Mark was a former ABC student and later faculty member at The Thacher School, teaching Russian language and working as the Assistant Director of Admission. In addition, he represented Ventura County as a Rotary Ambassadorial Scholar in Milan, Italy.

Mark and his wife, Cinzia Corio-Holman, have two children: Marco (aged 14) and Maya (age 10). The family resides in Portland, Oregon. They are all dual citizens of both the United States and Italy. They are all fluent in Italian.

OTHER PERTINENT INFORMATION

2010 – Present: Multnomah Athletic Club – Diversity Admissions Committee 2010

2011 – Present: Certified Compliance & Ethics Professional

2009 – Present: *Local Coordinator* for Department of State sponsored Student Exchange Program (makes weekly presentations to high school counselors and families about travel abroad programs, while developing marketing strategy for Oregon and Washington)

2004-2010: *Head of Finance Committee* of The Portland

International School (I make quarterly presentations about the state of the schools finance to parents and the Board of Trustees). Also, he led the Strategy Committee 2008-2009.

Mark Anthony Holman
Bonneville Power Administration
Equal Employment Compliance Specialist:
MBA, CCEP
503-230-3231

Other Books by Anointed Life Publishing

SKI

By A.L. Sutton

The war did not end for Ralph. It still resumes on even a small provocation: A tree line on a freeway instantly becomes a place where enemy fire erupts from, and rain brings back vivid memories of the horrors of war in the jungles of Vietnam. The pain is so intense that Ralph decides to do something that the very people he fought for will never forget. But despite the odds, Ralph discovers a more powerful weapon that will defeat all of his enemies and change his life forever.

DISCOVERING YOUR ANOINTING NUMBERS

By Carolyn Chambers

In her life-changing new book, Carolyn Chambers helps readers discover their anointing numbers and empower them to fight life's great battle-themselves. Simply put—everyone is at war with *self*. But walking anointed is something everyone can achieve. In, "Discovering Your Anointing Numbers: Allow me to introduce you to Yourself," Carolyn Chambers examines the influence that birth demographics have on human behavior. This is a compelling read for all.

THE ANOINTED LIFE- *Crucifying the Flesh*

By Carolyn Chambers
Thoughts received from the flesh alienate us from the grace of God; while those from the spirit bring righteousness, peace, and joy. The flesh cunningly attacks the will, the mind, and the emotions; keeping us in a place of immaturity and alienated from our inheritance through fear, doubt, and unbelief. But thoughts received from the spirit position us to live the anointed life—a life lived under the influence of the Holy Spirit. To get information regarding having Carolyn Chambers speak at your group, organization, or church, please e-mail us at: carolyn.allow@yahoo.com

PREPARING FOR PRIVATE AND PAROCHIAL SCHOOLS

By Winnie Eke, PhD.

This handbook is designed to help parents through the process of preparing themselves and their children for the challenges that lie ahead. It may not answer all the questions but it will highlight most of the common ones and those that I deem essential. It was inspired as a result of what I, as a parent, went through in the transition to an alternate educational experience with my own children.

We invite you to visit our website at:

Anointed Life Publishing

www.anointinglifepublishing.com